WRITTEN BY *NEW YORK TIMES* BESTSELLING
AUTHOR AND SINGER-SONGWRITER

JEWEL

Sweet Dreams

ILLUSTRATED BY

Amy June Bates

A PAULA WISEMAN BOOK
SIMON & SCHUSTER BOOKS FOR YOUNG READERS
New York   London   Toronto   Sydney   New Delhi

Simon & Schuster Books for Young Readers • An imprint of Simon & Schuster Children's Publishing Division • 1230 Avenue of the Americas, New York, New York 10020 • Text copyright © 2009 by WigglyToothMusic (ASCAP), administered by Downtown DLJ Songs (ASCAP) & Patrick Davis Music (BMI) / EMI Blackwood Music Inc. (BMI) • Illustrations copyright © 2013 by Amy June Bates • Based on the song "Sweet Dreams" in the album *Lullaby*. • All rights reserved, including the right of reproduction in whole or in part in any form. • SIMON & SCHUSTER BOOKS FOR YOUNG READERS is a trademark of Simon & Schuster, Inc. • For information about special discounts for bulk purchases, please contact Simon & Schuster Special Sales at 1-866-506-1949 or business@simonandschuster.com. • The Simon & Schuster Speakers Bureau can bring authors to your live event. For more information or to book an event, contact the Simon & Schuster Speakers Bureau at 1-866-248-3049 or visit our website at www.simonspeakers.com. • Book design by Laurent Linn • The text for this book is set in Worstveld Sling. • The illustrations for this book are rendered in chalk and gouache on chalkboard-painted paper. • Manufactured in China • 0913 SCP • 10 9 8 7 6 5 4 3 2 • Library of Congress Cataloging-in-Publication Data • Jewel, 1974– • Sweet dreams / Jewel ; illustrated by Amy June Bates. — 1st ed. • p. cm. • Summary: A parent who would do anything for a child lovingly urges him to fall into sweet dreams. • ISBN 978-1-4424-8931-8 (hardcover : alk. paper) — ISBN 978-1-4424-8932-5 (eBook) • [1. Lullabies. 2. Bedtime—Fiction. 3. Songs.] I. Bates, Amy June, ill. II. Title. • PZ8.3.J468Swe 2013 • 782.42—dc23 [E] • 2012045364

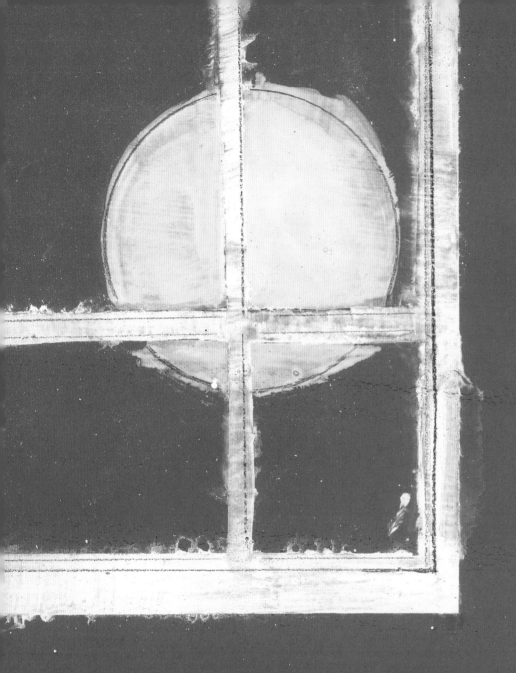

For my darling son, Kase,
who fills my heart with song
and my life with poetry
—JEWEL

For my grandma, sweet dreams
—AMY

The shadows are waltzing.

The moonbeams are calling.

Like a dream I am falling into

silver threads lined with dew.

Twinkling stars seem to shine just for you.

Behind your eyes are endless blue skies:

You travel places—

I want to come too.

Each breath that you breathe

is a brushstroke

It seems far away,
but there once was a day,
it was gray in a world without you.

To this heart, like a dove from above,
the miracle of your love found me.

So, sleep.
Fall into night's indigo hue.
Believe me, it's true.
There's nothing that I would not do,

for my dream
is sweet dreams for you.

So hushaby, and don't you cry.
Sweetly dream, little baby.

Yes, sleep.
Lose yourself in night's indigo hue.

Believe me, it's true.
There is nothing that
I would not do,

for my dream is sweet dreams . . .

Yes, my dream is sweet dreams for you